MICHAEL'S
GOLDEN RULES

HILLTOP ELEMENTARY SCHOOL

WRITTEN BY Deloris Jordan WITH Roslyn M. Jordan

INTRODUCTION BY Michael Jordan

ILLUSTRATED BY Kadir Nelson

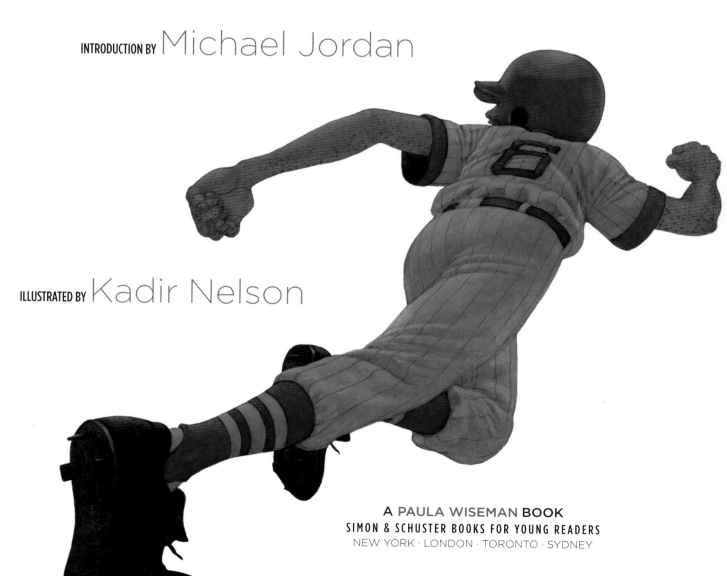

A PAULA WISEMAN BOOK
SIMON & SCHUSTER BOOKS FOR YOUNG READERS
NEW YORK · LONDON · TORONTO · SYDNEY

I dedicate this book to my grandchildren and to all youths. Even though you'll face the difficulties of today and tomorrow, still have a dream. Set goals, work to stay focused on your dreams, and work hard to achieve them. As you enjoy this life, love your family and contribute to others. Have patience. Be willing to understand others. Realize that no matter how hard you try, you'll never be the perfect person. Never give up without giving your best. Put in the work and the results will come. Being creative, consistent, and courageous, and having confidence in the good choices you make will direct your future.
—D. J.

For those who love to play baseball and have fun. Enjoy!
—R. M. J.

For my brothers and sisters, Saliha, Amin, Shedia, Jasmin, Samira, and Larry
—K. N.

SIMON & SCHUSTER BOOKS FOR YOUNG READERS
An imprint of Simon & Schuster Children's Publishing Division
1230 Avenue of the Americas, New York, New York 10020
Text copyright © 2007 by Deloris Jordan and Roslyn M. Jordan
Introduction copyright © 2007 by Michael Jordan
Illustrations copyright © 2007 by Kadir Nelson
All rights reserved, including the right of reproduction in whole or in part in any form.
SIMON & SCHUSTER BOOKS FOR YOUNG READERS is a trademark of Simon & Schuster, Inc.
Book design by Jessica Sonkin
The text for this book is set in New Caledonia.
The illustrations for this book are rendered in oils.
Manufactured in the United States of America
2 4 6 8 10 9 7 5 3 1
Library of Congress Cataloging-in-Publication Data
Jordan, Deloris.
Michael's golden rules / Deloris and Roslyn Jordan ; illustrated by Kadir Nelson.— 1st ed.
p. cm.
"A Paula Wiseman book."
Summary: Jonathan's friend Michael, Michael's parents, and Jonathan's family help him do his best in the Badgers' big baseball game.
ISBN-13: 978-0-689-87016-3 (isbn-13)
ISBN-10: 0-689-87016-7 (isbn-10)
[1. Baseball—Fiction. 2. Self-confidence—Fiction.] I. Jordan, Roslyn. II. Nelson, Kadir, ill. III. Title.
PZ7.J7622Mic 2006
[E]—dc22
2005016106

INTRODUCTION

As a small boy I had the great fortune of having parents who supported me and encouraged me to give my best. Before I excelled in basketball, I was aiming for no-hitters and home runs in baseball—my first love in sports.

As this story shares, in the summer, on weekends, and in the afternoons after school, my parents, two of my siblings, and I spent a great deal of time at the baseball field. My mother always says it was a way of keeping us involved and spending time together. For me, it was just fun.

Though I am more noted for my basketball abilities, there are some principles I learned back in those early days of playing baseball, principles that are essential to being a winner and that apply to every game, including the game of life. Some of these principles are highlighted in this book.

In reading this story, I recaptured those childhood moments when I played professional minor league baseball. That time for me was challenging in many ways, yet fulfilling. While I did not shine as many noted baseball players do, there was a light burning bright in my heart because I dared to give baseball a try. I did not do any great feats or leave behind any great notable moments, but when I stepped off the baseball field, I walked off a winner. This was because I gave it all I had for the time I was there, and I had fun.

Regardless of what game you endeavor to play, when it is over, if you know that you have put your heart into it, given your very best, and had fun along the way, you are a winner.

I've learned it takes heart to come out a winner every time, whether you win or lose.

MICHAEL JORDAN

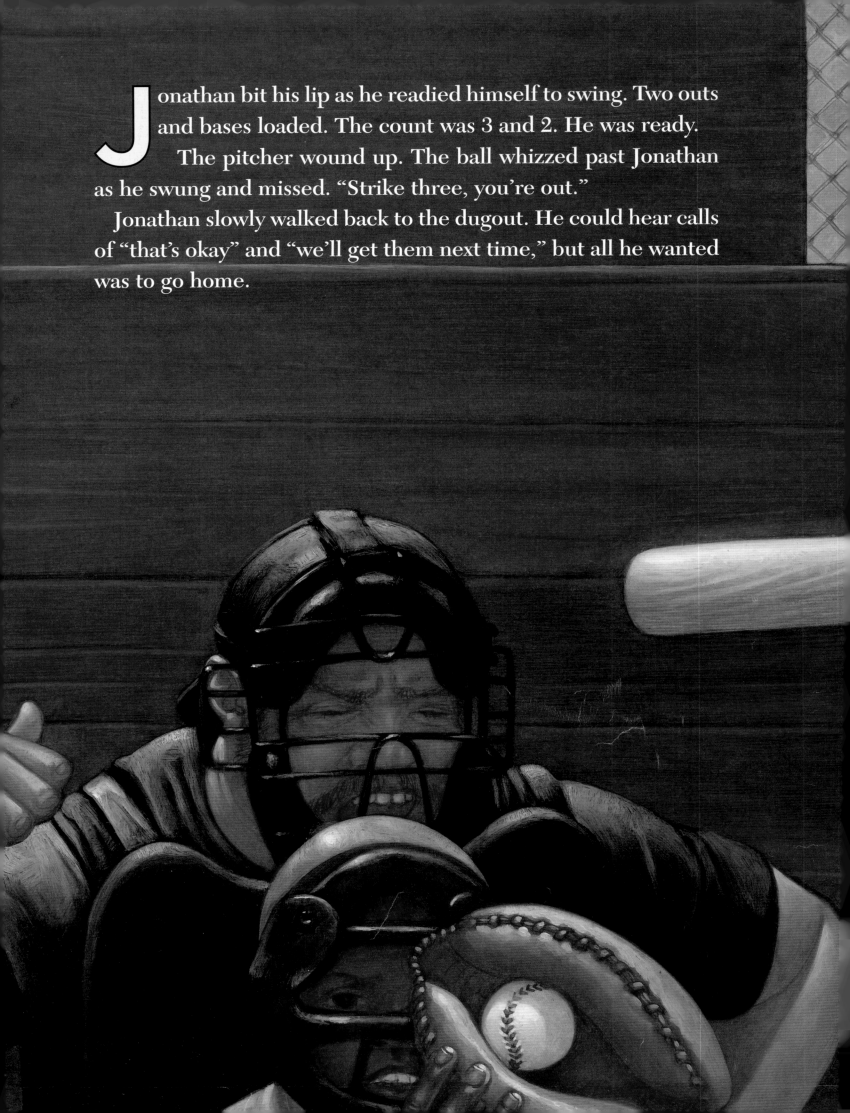

Jonathan bit his lip as he readied himself to swing. Two outs and bases loaded. The count was 3 and 2. He was ready.

The pitcher wound up. The ball whizzed past Jonathan as he swung and missed. "Strike three, you're out."

Jonathan slowly walked back to the dugout. He could hear calls of "that's okay" and "we'll get them next time," but all he wanted was to go home.

Jonathan walked home from the game with his best friend, Michael, and Michael's uncle Jack. Jonathan was glad Uncle Jack was here today, since Jonathan's mom had had to work.

"You boys played a good game."

Jonathan couldn't help saying, "But we lost. How could we have played a good game when we lost?"

"There's a lot more to a game than winning or losing, Jonathan. It's all about how you play the game. That's what makes a player great. That's what counts."

Jonathan was silent and Michael piped up. "Uncle Jack knows a lot about baseball. Uncle Jack, tell us about the ten golden rules of baseball. The ones you made up when you played in college. Please."

"Why don't you come by tomorrow, boys, and we can talk then."

Jonathan couldn't wait.

The next day, Saturday, Michael and Jonathan walked the few blocks from their neighborhood to Uncle Jack's house.

"Hi, boys. I'm glad you came by. I have my book here that Michael told you about—my book of golden rules. These got me through some tough games in school. Maybe they'll help you, too."

Michael and Jonathan read through the rules.

1. Know the game.
2. Pay attention to the coach at *all* times.
3. Know your opponent.
4. Be a team player.
5. Practice a winning attitude.
6. Find out what you do best.
7. Find out what you need to work on.
8. Practice, practice, practice.
9. Learn from your mistakes.
10. Have fun!

"Wow! Thanks, Uncle Jack!" said Michael.

Later in the afternoon Michael and Jonathan traded baseball cards.

"Wow, look, Michael!" shouted Jonathan. "Hank Aaron! He's awesome. He can hit a million home runs and steal a thousand bases! I'll bet he knows the golden rules of baseball."

"He sure plays like he does," said Michael. "I hope these rules will help us in the game tomorrow."

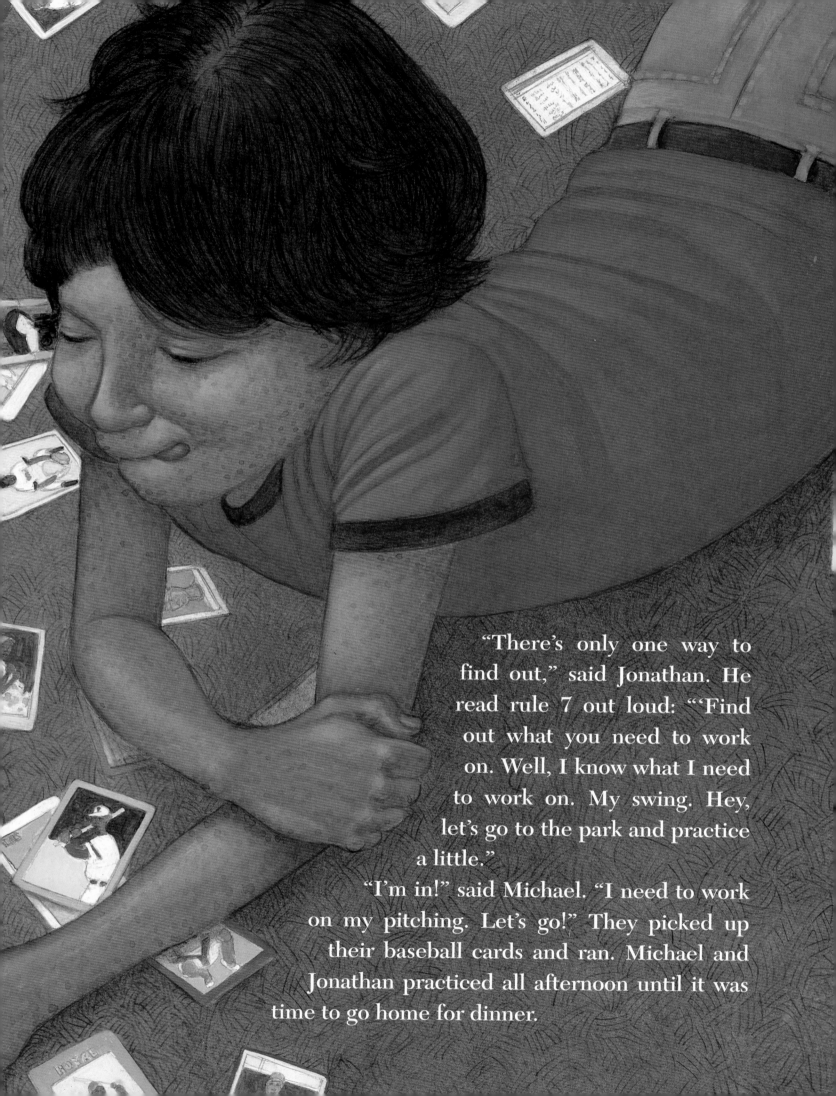

"There's only one way to find out," said Jonathan. He read rule 7 out loud: "'Find out what you need to work on. Well, I know what I need to work on. My swing. Hey, let's go to the park and practice a little."

"I'm in!" said Michael. "I need to work on my pitching. Let's go!" They picked up their baseball cards and ran. Michael and Jonathan practiced all afternoon until it was time to go home for dinner.

The next day was the big game.

"Hurry up, guys! It's time to go," Michael's papa yelled. "It's the big day. We're going to be late for the last game of the season!"

Inside the car, Michael said to Jonathan, "Man, wouldn't it be great if we made it to the play-offs? I can see it now: 'Badgers Make It to the Little League World Series.'"

"Yeah," Jonathan replied, wishing for a win, especially today. His mother was getting off work early to come to the game.

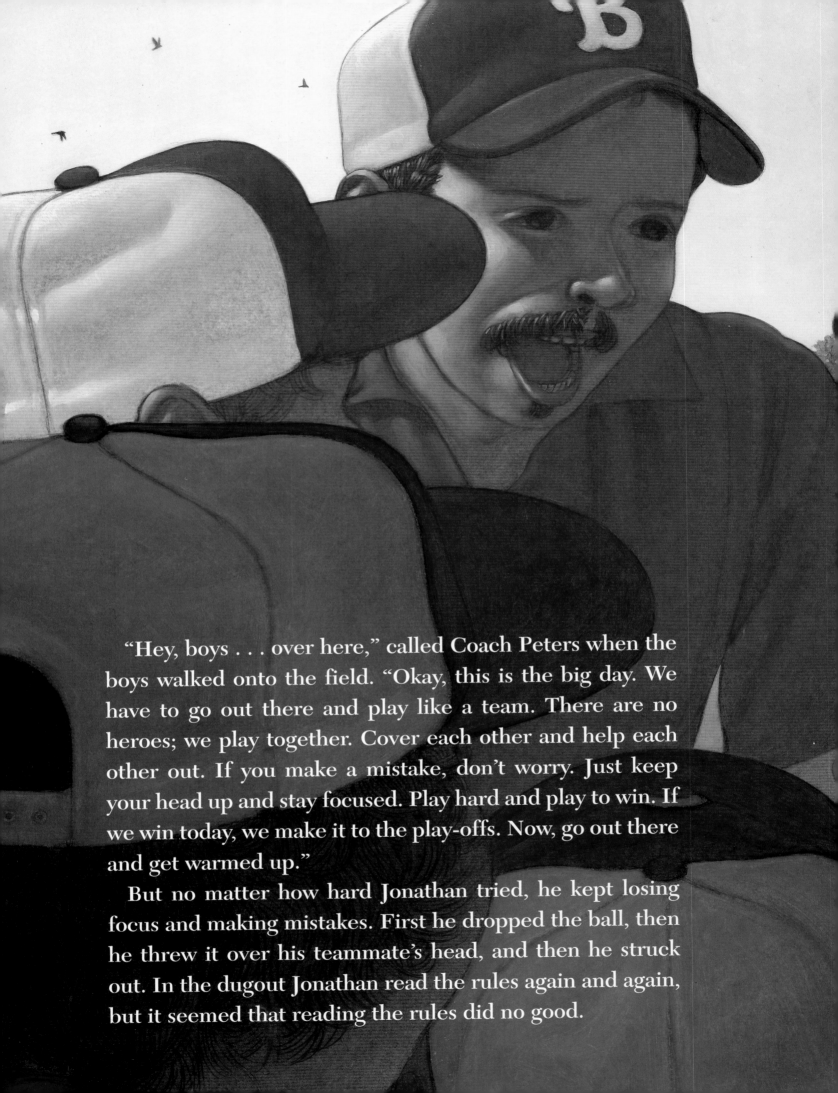

"Hey, boys . . . over here," called Coach Peters when the boys walked onto the field. "Okay, this is the big day. We have to go out there and play like a team. There are no heroes; we play together. Cover each other and help each other out. If you make a mistake, don't worry. Just keep your head up and stay focused. Play hard and play to win. If we win today, we make it to the play-offs. Now, go out there and get warmed up."

But no matter how hard Jonathan tried, he kept losing focus and making mistakes. First he dropped the ball, then he threw it over his teammate's head, and then he struck out. In the dugout Jonathan read the rules again and again, but it seemed that reading the rules did no good.

"Okay, guys, bring it in," Coach Peters called in the bottom of the second.

"Bobby, take shortstop. . . . Jonathan, you take third, and when I give you the signal, be ready to drop back and play deep. This kid always hits it down the third-base line," Coach said.

Jonathan had felt bad the week prior, when he had overheard Bobby, the team cocaptain and show-off, whisper, "C'mon, Coach, take him out of the game. He is always messing up."

Then Jonathan remembered the second golden rule: "Pay attention to the coach at *all* times."

"All right, Coach," Jonathan replied.

Just as Coach had said, the ball came Jonathan's way and Jonathan was in the right place to scoop it up and make the play. "Nice play, Jonathan!" shouted Michael from the mound.

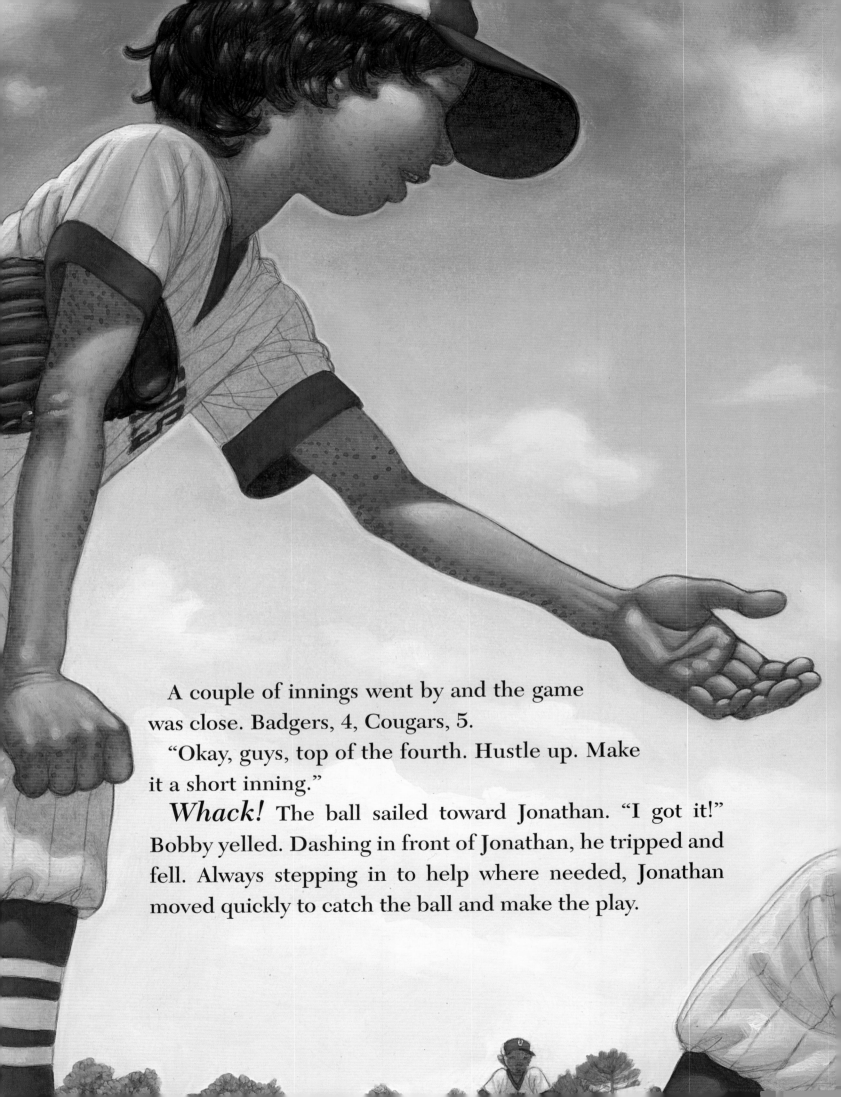

A couple of innings went by and the game was close. Badgers, 4, Cougars, 5.

"Okay, guys, top of the fourth. Hustle up. Make it a short inning."

Whack! The ball sailed toward Jonathan. "I got it!" Bobby yelled. Dashing in front of Jonathan, he tripped and fell. Always stepping in to help where needed, Jonathan moved quickly to catch the ball and make the play.

Turning to Bobby, Jonathan decided this would be a good time to put the team first rather than get back at Bobby for treating him so badly all the time. "Hey, Bobby, everyone makes mistakes. C'mon, let me help you up."

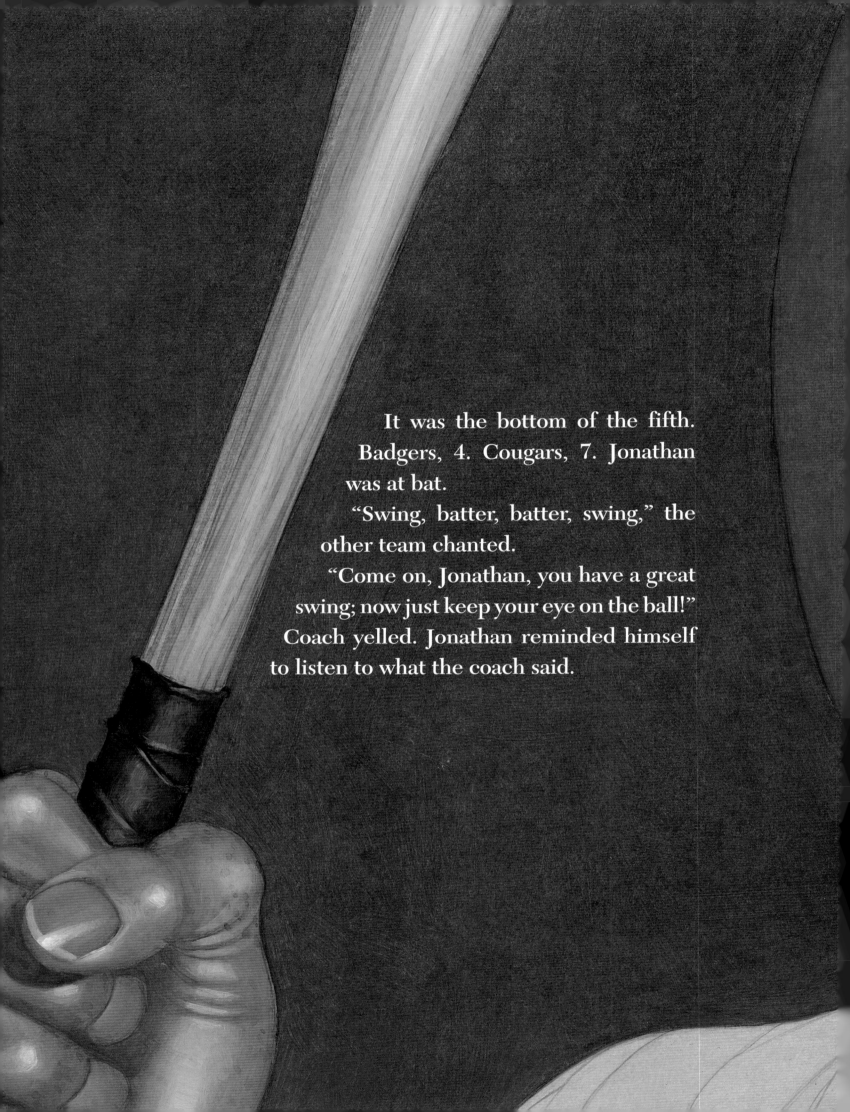

It was the bottom of the fifth. Badgers, 4. Cougars, 7. Jonathan was at bat.

"Swing, batter, batter, swing," the other team chanted.

"Come on, Jonathan, you have a great swing; now just keep your eye on the ball!" Coach yelled. Jonathan reminded himself to listen to what the coach said.

Smack! "Whoooaaa . . . way to go, Jonathan!" his teammates yelled. Jonathan got to first and brought in one run. Jonathan felt like he could do it again— even better. Practicing more had made a difference.

"Okay, boys, let's hold them to seven," Coach Peters said at the top of the sixth. "We still have a shot at winning."

"Yeah, if the benchwarmers stay on the bench where they belong," Bobby said under his breath so only Jonathan could hear.

Soon there were two outs, but the next pitch to the Cougars was a hit.

Whack! The ball flew high into the air over third base.

"Heads up, Jonathan; it's coming your way!" Coach yelled.

Moving to get under the ball, Jonathan told himself, "I can do it, I can do it." *Stay focused.*

Jonathan ran and stood under the ball with his arm raised. "Bobby, it's mine," he called.

The ball landed right in Jonathan's glove.

"You're out," he heard the umpire call. "That's the inning."

"Wow, good catch," said Bobby as he walked past Jonathan toward the dugout.

Jonathan smiled to himself, then answered, "Thanks, Bobby," and followed him to the dugout.

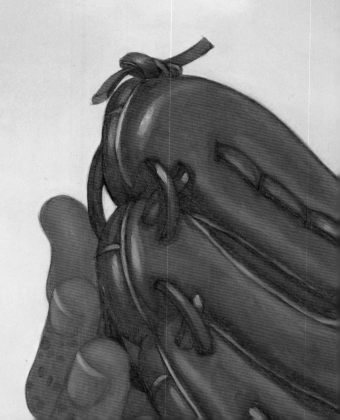

In the bottom of the last inning the Badgers gave it their all. Michael almost hit a home run with a man on first and second, but the Cougars' right fielder reached over the fence and grabbed it. Jonathan hit the ball to the Cougars' shortstop, who tagged the man on second heading to third, and on the last at bat,

Bobby grounded
out. The Badgers
had tried hard, but
they could not get past
the Cougars. The Cougars were on fire.
   The final score was Badgers, 5, and Cougars, 7. The Badgers
had lost, and the Cougars were going to the play-offs.

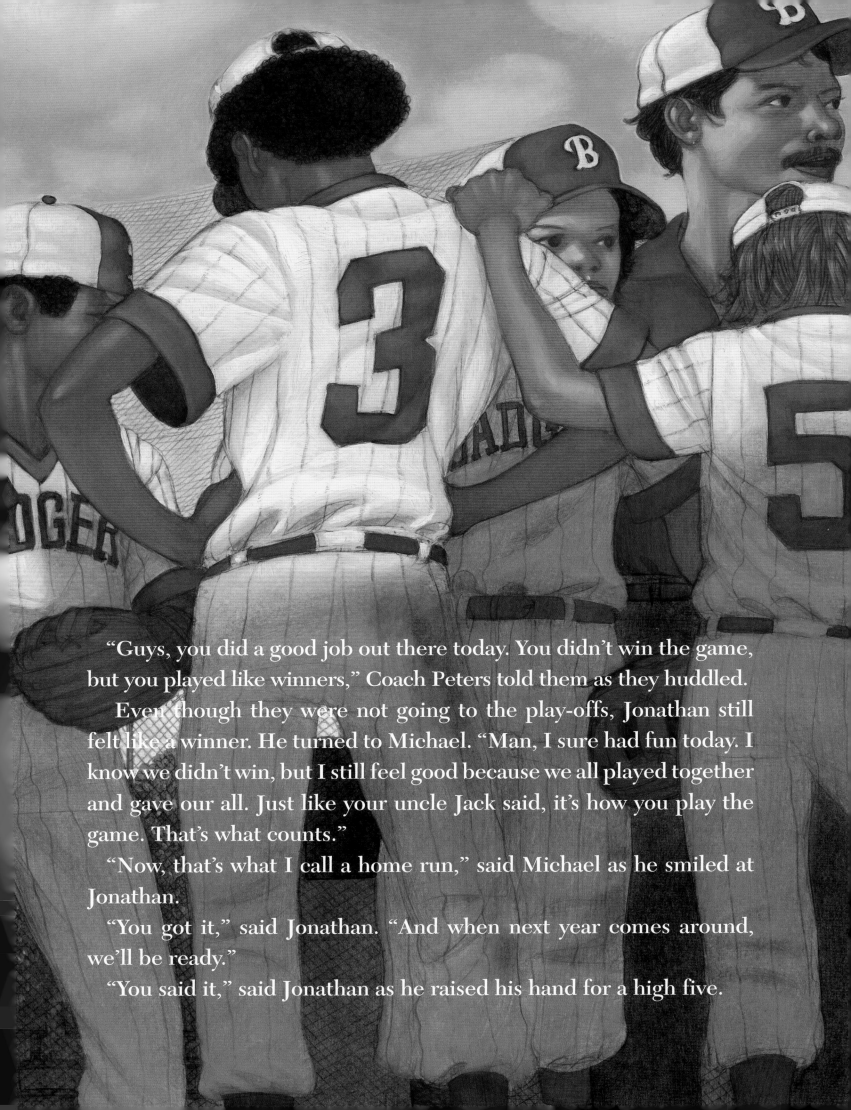

"Guys, you did a good job out there today. You didn't win the game, but you played like winners," Coach Peters told them as they huddled.

Even though they were not going to the play-offs, Jonathan still felt like a winner. He turned to Michael. "Man, I sure had fun today. I know we didn't win, but I still feel good because we all played together and gave our all. Just like your uncle Jack said, it's how you play the game. That's what counts."

"Now, that's what I call a home run," said Michael as he smiled at Jonathan.

"You got it," said Jonathan. "And when next year comes around, we'll be ready."

"You said it," said Jonathan as he raised his hand for a high five.

The Golden Rules

1. Know the game.
2. Pay attention to the coach at all times.
3. Know your opponent.
4. Be a team player.
5. Practice a winning attitude.
6. Find out what you do best.
7. Find out what you need to work on.
8. Practice, practice, practice.
9. Learn from your mistakes.
10. Have fun!